S0-BNE-381

KIDNAPPED BY VAMPIRES

D.E. DALY

An imprint of Enslow Publishing

WEST **44** BOOKS™

THE **Z** TEAM

WHEN ZOMBIES INVADE   GHOST TOWN
KIDNAPPED BY VAMPIRES WEREWOLVES ON THE LOOSE!

Please visit our website, www.west44books.com. For a free color catalog of all our high-quality books, call toll free 1-800-542-2595 or fax 1-877-542-2596.

Cataloging-in-Publication Data

Names: Daly, D.E.
Title: Kidnapped by vampires / D.E. Daly.
Description: New York : West 44, 2019. | Series: The Z team
Identifiers: ISBN 9781538381892 (pbk.) | ISBN 9781538381908 (library bound) | ISBN 9781538382950 (ebook)
Subjects: LCSH: Vampires--Juvenile fiction.
Classification: LCC PZ7.D359 Ki 2019 | DDC [E]--dc23

First Edition

Published in 2019 by
Enslow Publishing LLC
101 West 23rd Street, Suite #240
New York, NY 10011

Editor: Theresa Emminizer
Designer: Sam DeMartin

Printed in the United States of America

CPSIA compliance information: Batch #CS18W44: For further information contact
Enslow Publishing LLC, New York, New York at 1-800-542-2595.

THE Z TEAM

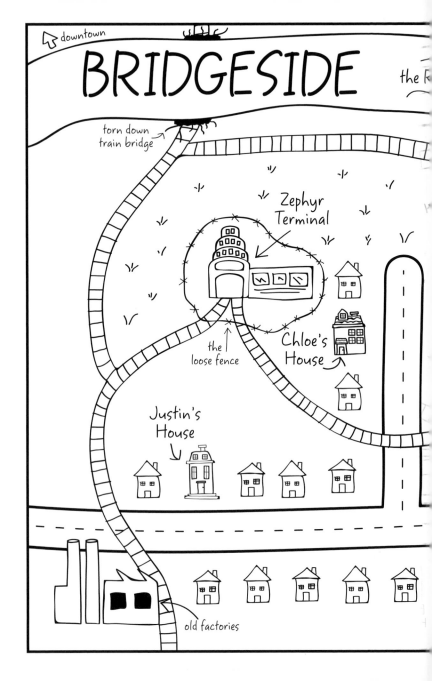

CHAPTER ONE
The Terminal Opens

*Z*ephyr Terminal stayed dark. Chloe checked from her window every night.

Just weeks ago, Chloe and her friends had snuck into the closed train station. They had tracked spooky sounds. A strange green light.

In the terminal's dispatch room, they'd turned a dial. A not-so-ghostly train showed up. Bringing a bunch of zombies to Bridgeside.

Chloe, Malik, and Justin sent the train back. All on their own. They'd decided to call themselves the Z Team. Ready for whatever came next.

But nothing else happened. Except September arrived. School. Homework.

The adventure might be over.

Chloe went to school bored as usual. Then in the hall—she saw it. A flyer, showing the terminal.

Colony Tours, it read. *New! See inside Zephyr Terminal! Learn history!*

Chloe grabbed the flyer off the wall. In homeroom, she showed her friends.

Justin loved history. He'd never heard of the company.

"Maybe they're from out of town," Justin said.

"We have to investigate," Chloe said. "The very first tour! Let's do it."

"We have homework," Malik said. "The tours are at night. My parents work then."

"My older sisters will take us!" Chloe said. "El loves any excuse to take the car."

Chloe reminded the boys: when they'd sent the zombies back by train…she'd seen three shadowy shapes jump off. Everything might be quiet, dark. But now this. Something was up.

She hoped.

On Thursday night, El and Em drove Chloe

and her friends to the terminal.

Seeing cars parked there was weird. The fence was open. Lights were on inside—normal lights.

"Whoa," El said, as she parked. "Look at that car!"

Chloe didn't see what made it so great. Old car. Black. Kind of flat, long.

Inside, a smiling old man sold them tickets and pointed  their way. The tour group was mostly teenagers. Some parents. One girl about ten. She was with a boy who looked like her. Probably her brother.

The tour guide was teenaged, too. Freckled face, big ears. Fast talker, with an Irish accent.

"This was a jewelry stand," the tour guide said, pointing. "Soldiers leaving by train could buy rings…"

Justin paid attention. Chloe looked around.

Last time she'd been here, zombies had filled the terminal.

"Are you babysitting?" a boy asked Em. The one with his sister. He wore a leather jacket.

"Here with my little sister," Em said.

"Oh." The boy glanced at Em's blonde hair. At Chloe's darker skin, dark curls. "Nice."

Chloe was adopted. Her sisters weren't.

It didn't matter, really. But sometimes Chloe wished other people could tell. Just by looking. That they all belonged together.

The tour went upstairs. The same steps where Chloe first faced a zombie.

Now it was just lights and the guide's stories.

In the familiar hallway—the dispatch room door was locked.

"That room's not safe," the tour guide explained.

The Z Team traded looks. Not safe was right.

Nothing exciting happened all tour.

But at the end, a teenage girl said, "Has anyone seen my friends? My cell phone's not working!"

The Z Team traded looks again. Their phones hadn't worked in the terminal last time.

The boy who Em talked to *the whole time* looked around, too. "Maria?" he said.

He hadn't done a good job watching his sister.

"Let's go," El said.

The freckled tour guide walked out at the same time. He headed to the car El liked.

"One sec," El said to them. She suddenly wasn't in such a hurry. "Hey, cool car!"

While El talked to the guide, Chloe watched the terminal.

The boy with the leather jacket walked out—with the little girl. He'd found her.

The teenager missing her friends walked out crying. She hadn't found them.

"Look," Chloe said.

"Look!" Justin said, too. Pointing up.

Chloe looked. With the inside lights and car headlights on—she could see shapes overhead.

Bats circled Zephyr Terminal.

CHAPTER TWO
Monster Math

At lunchtime in school, everyone talked about the missing high schoolers. Two from the tour. Two more in town over the weekend.

Malik worked on his math homework. He still hadn't finished. It was due next period.

"I hear cops are searching the terminal," Justin said.

"Em and El think it's some prank," Chloe said. "Or a dare, to sneak away."

"Missing high schoolers," Justin said quietly. "Shadowy, fast shapes. *Bats*. Seen all over town, since Thursday."

Malik focused on his worksheet.

"Lights and people at the terminal scared out some bats roosting there," he said. "That's what everyone thinks."

"Everyone except us," Justin said. "What would it be in a movie?"

The zombies hadn't been like the movies. Malik shrugged.

"*Malik!*" Chloe said.

"Vampires," Malik said. "You're thinking vampires came to town on the Eerie Express."

"Duh," Chloe said. "The three shadowy shapes." She pointed at Malik's worksheet. "That math's wrong."

Malik started erasing.

"Three vampires," Justin said. "Can't be as bad as tons of zombies, right?"

Malik wasn't so sure about that math, either.

"Let's talk after school, okay?" Malik said. "Come over to my house."

Malik's concrete basement wasn't the coolest headquarters. But it worked for after-school research.

Justin tried to find a website for Colony Tours. "Everything has a website," he insisted.

But—nothing.

Chloe made a list of everything they knew about vampires.

"Stakes, garlic, fangs, no sunlight—yup," Malik said. "But accents? Leather jackets?"

"Vampires on *Sunny the Monster Masher* always have those!"

"My dad has an accent and a leather jacket," Malik said. "Is he a suspected vampire?"

Chloe grinned.

"What?" Malik said.

"I love that we get to say things like 'suspected vampires' and stuff," She said.

Malik rolled his eyes. "You'll be sorry when they drink your blood." He added "no reflection" and "old but sometimes young-looking" to the list.

"Your sisters talked to those guys," Justin said to Chloe. "One with an accent. One with a leather jacket."

"Those guys were around the whole time!" Malik said.

"Are we sure?" Justin said. "If they move that fast?"

"I'll see what I can find out when El picks me up," Chloe said. She started a new list: *Suspected Vampires!*

When it was time for Chloe and Justin to head home, Chloe was barely in her sister's car a minute. She came running back.

"Leather jackets!" she said, upset. "Accent!"

"What?" Justin said. His dad's car pulled up, honking.

"I just heard—*Emily* made plans with that leather jacket-wearing boy! *Ellen's* meeting up with the tour guide!" Malik had never heard Chloe use her sisters' full names before. "They have dates Friday! With our *suspected vampires*!"

She didn't seem to enjoy saying those words this time.

CHAPTER THREE
Garlic Breath

We have to date crash.

JG

Justin waited for a response from the Z Team group message. He was listening to his favorite history podcast's vampire episodes. About spooky history. Like Vlad the Impaler. Or a never-aging count, from France—spotted decades after he "died."

Justin kept picturing Count von Count from *Sesame Street*. Maybe because *Sesame Street*'s version of a vampire was always counting. Teaching kids numbers. Justin was working on math homework while listening.

Justin was fine at math. But the new teacher gave a lot of homework.

MY SISTERS WOULD BE SO MAD.

Do you want them turned into vampires?

His brother Charlie stuck his head into Justin's room. "Hey, nerd. Want to watch a movie?"

"What?" Justin took off his headphones.

"Never mind," Charlie said. He started to close the door.

"No, I heard you. I was just…surprised. That'd be cool."

Charlie had been turned into a living zombie. Only for about a day. Charlie didn't remember anything. The Z Team had found a cure in time.

Vampires, though…Justin found nothing about vampire cures. Vampires were stuck. Vampires were forever.

He glanced at his phone.

Better make a plan. How's research going?

"Can it be a vampire movie?" Justin asked Charlie.

Charlie shrugged. "Don't care."

By date night, the Z Team had assembled all their notes. Plus weapons for fighting vampires. Ones that could fit in jackets or pockets.

Justin hadn't been able to get holy water. They didn't exactly sell bottles at church. Malik mentioned "Zamzam water," from a holy well in Mecca. But that was even harder to get.

Justin read, though, that vampires couldn't cross running water. Maybe they were weak against water in general.

He passed out bottles of pure spring water. Pieces of garlic he'd put in each bottle bobbed around.

They'd all eaten garlic pizza for dinner. Armed with garlic breath and permission from Malik's mom, they walked up Long Street. To the Mud Stop—the town coffee shop. Where high schoolers went. There wasn't really anywhere else in Bridgeside to go.

It was mostly dark. The streetlights were on.

Sunset colors still haunted the sky.

El was outside the Mud Stop, waiting by her car.

"What're you doing?" she asked them.

"Getting hot chocolate," Chloe said. "Where's your *date*?"

"Francis?" El said.

"*Francis*?" Malik repeated. A little old-fashioned for a guy's name.

"He's late," El said. She checked the time. "He doesn't have a phone, so…"

"Everyone has a cell phone!" Chloe said.

"He just moved from another country, Chloe," El said. "He doesn't have a phone that works *here* yet."

Inside, Em's date carried coffees over to her. He smiled. Very white teeth. Sharp-looking.

Justin nudged Chloe.

"Don't get in Francis's car!" Chloe told El. "He's a stranger!"

"Who's the older sister here?" El said. She laughed and waved the Z Team off.

Em made a go-away face the second they walked in.

"Em!" Chloe said, rushing up. "Let's take a picture together!"

"What?!" Em said.

"This is your other sister, right?" leather-jacket boy said. He smiled wider. "I'm Lucas."

Chloe went to shake his hand. On purpose, she spilled her garlic water. All over his leather jacket.

"Sorry!" Chloe said. Holding up her phone, she said, "You can be in the picture, too. Selfie!"

"You're being so weird," Em moaned. Her date blinked as the phone flashed.

"Little sisters usually are," he said. He brushed the spilled water off.

"How's your sister?" Chloe said. Justin and Malik stood nearby, trying to breathe garlic in Lucas's direction.

"My sister?" Lucas repeated. He blinked harder.

"From the tour?" Justin said. "Maria, right?"

"Maria? That's…not my sister's name…"

"Girl with you on the tour?" Malik prompted. "About ten. Looked like you."

Lucas rubbed his head. "Huh," he said.

"Where did Francis take my sister?"

"I don't care what Francis does!" Maria said. "Francis is an idiot! Francis is only seventy!"

"Ew!" Chloe said. Her sister was on a date with a seventy-year-old! Somehow that seemed weirder than him being two hundred or something.

The dumpster rattled.

Maria managed to pry Chloe's hands off her hair. She was much stronger than Chloe. Malik threw his garlic water at her—the last bottle.

Maria stumbled back, her hair and face soaked.

"I'll drain you all," she hissed, fangs showing. "You wait!"

The dumpster lid burst open. A whole flock of bats streamed out. Many brushed right against Chloe. She covered her hair.

The Z Team ran for cover. The bats circled them. Chloe ran back toward the street—trying to get the bats to follow to the Mud Spot. If Em saw, she'd know it was all real.

But the bats just flew away. And there was

CHAPTER FOUR
Don't Split Up

The good news: one sister was dating a real boy.

The bad news: the other left with a vampire.

Chloe tried calling El and sending her the picture Justin took. No answer.

"If she's driving, she wouldn't answer," Justin said. "It doesn't mean something bad happened."

"It doesn't mean something bad *didn't*," Malik said.

"Not helping," Chloe told them. She ran back into Mud Spot.

"El left with a vampire," she announced to Em and her date. "Do something!"

"Someone dressed like a vampire?" Lucas

He was talking to El.

"Very," she said. Francis handed her the keys. She got in the driver's seat.

"I'm telling mom," Chloe hissed. El started the car.

Malik turned on the flash on his WowNow. Francis covered his eyes. He hopped into the car. Justin snapped a picture with his phone. Flash on, too.

"Don't be so immature!" El said. Then she drove off. With Francis.

Justin looked at his phone. "Chloe, you better see this."

The picture showed El in the car. Only El. Francis's seat appeared empty.

They'd found one vampire.

"Maybe I headed that soccer ball too hard at practice…"

"You play soccer?!" Em said. "For Lakeview High?" They started talking about school sports.

Chloe motioned the boys to see her phone picture. Lucas showed up normally in the selfie. His teeth didn't look sharp in the picture. Just slightly crooked.

"Do phone cameras count as mirrors?" Chloe asked.

Justin didn't know.

"I've got my WowNow." Malik held up his action camera. "I'll try filming."

"Better start quick," Justin said.

The freckled tour guide was out front. He'd parked his old black car. The top was down. A convertible. El was checking it out.

They rushed back out.

"I remember you all," the tour guide said. Francis's smile was big. Friendly. Normal teeth. "Did you enjoy the terminal?"

"No," Chloe said.

"Guess I better keep practicing the tour," Francis said. "You ready to go?"

no sign of Maria.

"You look that way, I'll go this way!" Chloe said.

"Splitting up is always a bad idea!" Malik shouted.

Chloe was already heading to check by the next building. No sign of Maria there. All dark for the night.

"Your friend's right," a voice said behind her. Irish accent.

Chloe knew before she turned. Francis.

Despite his freckles and big ears, he looked very serious.

"Splitting up *is* always a bad idea," he said.

"I know what you are," Chloe said. She held her phone camera up. "I'm going to prove it."

She turned on flash.

He put on sunglasses. And walked toward her.

"No, you're not," he said. Almost sadly.

Chloe never liked TV characters who screamed all the time. But her friends needed to know she was in trouble.

She screamed as loud as she could.

CHAPTER FIVE
A Missing Friend

Justin and Malik were checking out the dumpster the bats had come from—when Chloe screamed.

They both sprinted in that direction.

No one was around when they got there. No sign of Chloe.

Malik called her. It went to voicemail.

They came around the front. And there was El, by her own car.

"You're back!" Justin said. "From your date."

"We just drove around," El said. "It wasn't really a date—"

"Chloe's gone!" Malik said.

"Yeah," El said, "I got her text." She waved

her phone at them.

> Just left with Hallie! Going to stay at her house again! Didn't want you to worry!

"*Hallie?*" Malik said.

"Her best friend," El said. Looking at their faces, she said, "Okay, her best girl friend. They have sleepovers all the time."

"The vampires must have Chloe's phone!" Justin whispered to Malik.

"Can't tell her that," Malik whispered back. "Sounds made up."

Em came out of Mud Spot, frowning. "Did you get this text?" she asked El.

Her date Lucas followed. "Didn't you want to go on a walk?"

"Walk where?" Em said.

"Just—that way? In the moonlight?" Lucas said. He seemed a little lost.

"Maybe you did hit your head too hard," Em said.

"Em," Malik tried. "Chloe's been kidnapped."

"Whoa," Em said. "Hallie didn't *kidnap* her. I'm sorry my sister went with her other friend,

23

but…"

"Some kids from our school are actually missing right now," El said. "Don't even joke."

Malik threw up his hands. Teenage girls. They weren't going to listen to him.

"Where did Francis go?" Justin demanded. "Where does he live?"

El ignored him. Her phone beeped again. "See, she's fine," she said to Em. "Bye, boys."

They were left standing there.

Lucas, too.

Malik had an idea.

"You know what we never talked about?" Malik said to Justin. "Vampires hypnotizing people. Usually it's girls in Dracula movies, but—"

"Lucas seems pretty hypnotized," Justin agreed. He paused. "Do you think vampires hypnotized Chloe?"

"Nah," Malik said. He tried to sound sure. Still, he couldn't picture Chloe listening to any vampire. She didn't like to be told what to do.

Lucas wandered off. Hands in his jacket pockets. Staring up.

A lone bat moved against the clouds.

CHAPTER SIX
Think Fast

Justin searched on his phone as they walked. They needed better weapons.

They'd laid out the broken hockey stick at his house. It was too big and obvious to carry into Mud Spot. But it might work as a stake. They'd used it against the zombies.

Well. Chloe had.

"Do you have any real silver?" Justin asked Malik.

Malik shook his head.

Justin's house didn't have a single real silver fork. His mom maybe had silver jewelry, but at her city apartment. Justin only went there every other weekend.

"If we could only trap them in sunlight," Justin said. "That would get rid of them." Checking a new list of vampire weaknesses, he saw celery and onions were on there, too. "Maybe more vegetables?"

He almost tripped, walking while looking at his phone. Malik grabbed his arm in time.

"Wait, vegetables," Justin said. "My brother Charlie has a potato gun!"

Malik thought he'd seen a potato gun at a science fair. "Like a cannon, shoots a whole potato?"

"I wish it was a cannon," Justin said. "It's like a little red gun. You press it against a potato, then it makes a little pellet. Three hundred shots from one potato!" His dad had hidden it months ago. Since Charlie kept shooting pellets at Justin.

"We should get it," Justin said. "We could shoot garlic, instead." They had garlic in their pockets. More at Justin's house.

"We need to follow him," Malik said. Ahead, Lucas kept walking. Hopefully leading toward Chloe. "And we shouldn't split up."

They decided to see where Lucas went. Then go back, get anything they could. Return for Chloe.

Lucas turned off Long Street. Away from lights. Out onto the grass. Where the broken train tracks looped.

"He's turning toward the old factories," Justin said. The factories were all closed, mostly empty. But one or two buildings over there were still in use. Some were being torn down, really unsafe. If they weren't supposed to go into the terminal alone, they really, really weren't supposed to be near the old factories. He'd heard from Charlie that some high-schoolers got arrested for partying there.

"If I was a vampire in Bridgeside," Malik said, "I'd hide out in the factories. Lots of dark, empty areas to hide from the sun."

"And hide kidnapped high schoolers," Justin said. One middle schooler, too.

They decided Justin better call his dad about staying at Malik's. Malik told his parents he was staying over at Justin's.

Morning was far away. And this could take a while.

CHAPTER SEVEN
Worst Vampire Ever

Being grabbed and carried by a vampire who could run really, really fast wasn't good for a stomach full of pizza.

Chloe threw up a little over Francis's shoulder. He dropped her, covering his nose.

Chloe felt terrible, but the good news—her vomit smelled like garlic.

"Ha," she said.

Francis bent over, looking ready to throw up, too.

"Would you vomit blood?" Chloe asked. She was so curious, she couldn't help herself.

"So gross," Francis said, gagging. "How

come you're not running?"

Because Chloe knew exactly where she was. She could hear the river. She saw the factories ahead. She was standing on broken train tracks.

"Run where?" she said. "Don't you have superspeed?"

"Not exactly super," Francis said.

"Besides, you kidnapped my sister," Chloe said.

"I did not," Francis said. "I haven't kidnapped anyone but you. That's all Maria and Arnold."

"Maria's the vampire girl? She's not Lucas' sister?"

"Lucas is the boy she hypnotized?" Francis asked. He stood up straight again. "Nope. She just picked him out because they looked alike. She could hang around the tour. Or the pizza place. Or the coffee shop. A kid alone attracts attention. But people see her with a boy with the same color hair…and they just assume. Humans are always making assumptions."

"True," Chloe said. "So where's El? You didn't bite her?"

"No!" Francis said. "That is, not yet. Do you think she'd let me?"

"NO!"

"You seem sure…Did she say something?" He ruffled his hair. So it covered his ears more.

Chloe crossed her arms. "My sister does *not* date vampires. Plus you're too old. Maria said you're *seventy*."

"I've been on the other side of the portal since I was turned!" Francis said. "Time's different there, and we just came back. I'm practically still seventeen!"

"The portal?" Chloe said.

"Where did you think the trains were coming from?" Francis said. "Weren't you the ones who opened the portal? I heard you were."

"Heard from who?" Chloe asked quickly.

Francis opened his mouth, then shut it. Chloe saw fangs for a second. Those hadn't been part of his smile before.

"The witch?" Chloe asked. They'd heard the witch's voice on the radio in the dispatch room. They knew she'd controlled the zombies. "Is she in charge of you, too?"

"No," Francis said. "But Arnold made a deal with her. We set up our own food supply in Bridgeside. And we help with her plan to get through the portal."

"Arnold…he's the third vampire?" Chloe asked.

Francis waved at the air. "If we're going to talk, can we at least move away from the smell?"

They stepped closer to the river.

"I heard vampires had a problem with running water," Chloe said. Maybe she could get some information out of him. She didn't think vampires were very chatty. But then, Francis had talked all tour.

"Crossing it," Francis said. "We can't leave Bridgeside that way. We could go on the bridge, but…" He changed the subject, pointing at the terminal in the distance. Its normal lights glowed. "I fixed those lights myself, you know."

"I didn't know," Chloe said. "Or about the portal. What's it like on the other side?"

"Miserable," Francis said. "It's all our kind. Monster types. Whoever built that terminal—it was a trap. Back when the trains passed through. Any time something supernatural rode a train into Zephyr Terminal? Wham, other side. The portal captured all the witch's zombie trains. Then I guess it captured her."

He shivered. "I'd only been a vampire for a few months," he said. "I was trying to take a train to New Orleans. I heard that's the best place for vampires. So I hid my car, in case I came back. Got on a train. And wham!"

"Good," Chloe said. "You haven't been able to drink anybody's blood, then. For like fifty years."

"I wasn't going to drink anybody's blood without asking," he said. "That's rude."

Chloe stared at his friendly, freckled face and fangs.

"Francis," she said, "are you maybe terrible at being a vampire?"

He looked hurt. Then he sighed. "I am, yeah."

"Maybe you could just let me go?" Chloe

suggested. She crossed her fingers behind her back, to lie. "I'll tell my sister how great you are?"

"I could," Francis said. He tilted his head. "You'll just pretend you don't know about vampires? About the kidnapped high schoolers? Go back to your normal life, and let the police look?"

"Are they all still alive? Did you turn them into vampires?" Chloe asked.

"Arnold and Maria don't want more vampires," Francis said. "They want snacks. Alive, trapped snacks. So there's always more blood."

Chloe couldn't even manage to lie. "The Z Team will stop that."

"The Z Team?" Francis repeated. "Ha. We'll see."

CHAPTER EIGHT
The Real Villains

"Should we be doing something?" Malik whispered to Justin.

The little vampire girl, Maria, had met Lucas in front of the factories. She hummed and waved her fingers at his eyes.

Then she started drinking blood from Lucas's wrist. He just stood there in his leather jacket, looking confused.

"Next time, bring me another teenager like I told you," Maria said. She stood on her tiptoes to stare at Lucas's eyes. Then she shoved him.

"Huh," Lucas said. He stumbled away.

Malik and Justin crept closer.

"I smell garlic," Maria said. She sped after Lucas. "Did you eat garlic?"

Malik and Justin crept back, further into the bushes.

"Let's get that garlic gun," Malik said. They weren't far from Justin's house—he lived closest to the factories. Near the tracks that looped around Bridgeside.

"No new victims for us?" a voice said.

That was a movie-villain voice. High, cold. Somehow smart-sounding. No, not smart. Like he *thought* he was smarter than everybody else. Much tougher-sounding than a ten-year-old vampire.

Malik stopped and looked back. It was the old man from the tour—the one who'd smiled and sold tickets.

"We have five," Maria said. "Counting Lucas."

"But Francis isn't dining with us yet," the other vampire said. "Once he starts taking his share, we'll need more."

"Francis should get his own blood," Maria whined. "He isn't helping."

"Guiding the tours was the distraction

we required."

"He just likes talking!"

The older vampire sniffed, loudly. "I smell garlic," he said.

It was really hard not to run. But Malik and Justin kept sneaking, quietly. Running was too loud.

They made it to Justin's. In the

sniff

garage, they found Charlie's potato gun hidden on a high shelf. Malik, tall for his age, stood on a stool and got it. When they tested it on garlic, it couldn't pull out a whole pellet like from a potato. The garlic was thicker. It shot little chunks, but not too hard or fast.

Malik's WowNow had been filming the whole time. But when they checked the video—nothing. It captured only their surroundings. Only their own voices.

Malik just couldn't seem to record supernatural stuff. His best skill was useless.

"If we don't save Chloe soon, I'm not going to have enough time to study for the math quiz

Monday," Malik said.

"Really?" Justin said.

"I'll fail! My parents will kill me! Well, not really. They'll be disappointed. That's worse."

"What's worse is vampires really killing us," Justin said.

Malik picked up the broken hockey stick. He stepped on it and pulled, hard. It snapped again. He handed one half to Justin. So they both had a sharp end.

"Unless we get them first," Malik said.

CHAPTER NINE
The Count

"We should attack at dawn!" Malik said.

"We don't know if they sleep during the day," Justin said. "What if they don't? They could still be faster, stronger. Just indoors."

"Don't you want to save Chloe?" Malik said.

"Just let me keep looking," Justin said. Think, he told himself. With the zombies, he'd found a zombie museum's website. They'd learned a weird thing about real zombies: they were scared of frogs. The zombie museum had been in New Orleans. He tried searching for it online.

Nothing.

But there was a vampire shop. The only

vampire shop in the country. It had a website.

"I told you everything has a website," Justin said. "This sells a vampire-hunting kit!"

"Order it!" Malik said.

Justin shook his head. "How fast do you think that would get here?" He looked at the list. "It's mostly stuff we could get, anyway. Stakes, mirrors, garlic…wait. Mustard seeds? Why mustard seeds?"

"Vampires are allergic to mustard?" Malik said hopefully.

Justin searched "mustard seeds + vampire." A vampire myth came up. He read aloud, "For protection, sprinkle mustard seeds around your door. A vampire will have to count each one—"

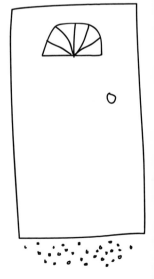

"Count?" Malik repeated.

Justin's phone was running slow. He made Malik pull his out to search, too.

"This is why Count von Count on *Sesame Street* is always counting things," Justin said, as they read. He couldn't believe it. "I thought it was just funny. But it's based on a real vampire legend." That was so nerdy. He loved it.

"You keep them counting until the sun comes up," Malik said. "Boom! Now…where do we get mustard seeds?"

"It doesn't have to be that kind. They have to count anything," Justin said. He looked around the garage. He spotted a bag. "Birdseed! Let's do this!"

"But first, high-five," Malik said, holding his hand up. "Now let's save Chloe!"

CHAPTER TEN
Tour Guide

"You brought a middle schooler?" the old vampire said. He looked down his nose at Chloe. He smiled, scarily friendly. "Francis. You know when it's teenagers, we can get away with this longer. Especially when we pick troublemaking teenagers."

Chloe guessed this was Arnold. He reminded her of a jerky principal.

"My mistake," Francis said. "Oh well. I'll just put her in with the others."

"Hypnotize her to forget," Arnold said. "Then send her back. Humans get upset about missing children much too quickly."

"She's eaten garlic," Francis said. "Once it's out of her system—then, of course."

Arnold's lip curled. Showing his fangs. "Fine."

Francis took Chloe to the factory room where the four high school students were tied up.

"I'm just tying her up," he called. He didn't. He gave Chloe a fist bump before closing the door on her.

Chloe ran to undo the knots holding the high-schoolers. They all seemed sleepy. She tapped the face of the first girl.

Then she heard a noise. Bats' wings. All rising up at once.

Someone was coming. The bats were reacting.

"Maria," Arnold's voice called. "Go stop them."

Chloe couldn't believe she was missing this. She heard shouting—Malik and Justin. Sticks clashing. An "ow!" from Maria.

"Wait until we're inside!" Justin's voice called. "We have to get them all at once!"

Chloe stopped trying the knots. "All at once"

included Francis.

She went to the door and banged on it. "Let me out!" she said.

From the other side came a sound like rain. No, more like a rainstick. A lot of little things falling and sliding.

The door yanked open.

Malik and Justin stood there. They were sweaty. Holding broken hockey sticks, birdseed bags, and what looked like a red toy gun.

All three vampires were on their hands and knees picking up birdseed. Birdseed was everywhere.

"What's this?" Chloe asked her friends.

"It's a rescue!" Malik said.

"Get this: they can't help it, they have to count!" Justin said. "Actually, I better finish the birdseed trail." He ran to sprinkling more birdseed—leading right out the door.

"We got our bikes and trailed birdseed here. All the way from the bridge!" Malik said. "If we connect the trail up, they'll have to follow it there."

"To the bridge?"

"They're weaker by running water. So

hopefully that'll slow their counting, until the sun comes up!"

"Yes!" Chloe said. Then she looked over at Francis. His mouth moved as he counted silently. "But not Francis."

"*Not Francis?*" Malik said.

Chloe went over, careful to step nowhere near Arnold or Maria. She shook Francis' shoulder. He kept counting. She tugged his arm. He kept counting. She yanked harder. He snarled. And kept counting.

"Help me!" she told Malik.

"Is this the thing where the kidnappee sides with the kidnapper?" he asked.

"Just trust me!"

Malik came over. Together, they tugged Francis away from the seeds. He tried to turn back. Chloe jumped in his path.

"What's going on?" Justin asked, walking back in.

"Just count me," Chloe said to Francis. "How many Chloes are there?"

"…One," Francis said.

"How many sisters do I have?"

"Two."

"How many people on the Z Team?"

Francis looked at all three of them and smiled. One fang poked over his lip.

"Is this working?" Chloe asked.

"Seems so," Francis said. He put his hands to his face. Blocking his side vision. "I better not look at the seeds again."

"What's the thing called," Malik asked Justin, "where kidnappees side—"

"He's not a bad vampire," Chloe interrupted. "He's just Francis. Francis, tell them your most evil plan."

"…What, getting a human girlfriend? Who'll let me have human blood sometimes?"

"That's your most evil plan?" Justin asked. "Get a girlfriend?"

Francis shrugged. "It makes sense, doesn't it?"

"Oh, brother," Malik said. "He is bad at being a vampire. Is that even a real accent?"

"It is too," Francis said. "Francis MacGillicuddy, of County Kerry. Until I caught a vampire feeding on the family cows."

"I think we should keep him," Chloe said to Justin and Malik.

"A pet vampire?" Justin said.

"Can we have a vampire cow instead?" Malik asked.

"The cows weren't vampires," Francis tried explaining. "It's not only biting that turns someone. The high schoolers will be fine. I can de-hypnotize them for you."

Maria and Arnold both crawled outside. Still counting.

"You'll pay," Arnold snarled. "You'll all… twelve hundred sixteen, no, twelve hundred fifteen—"

The Z Team walked Francis out. Keeping him away from the birdseed.

"Vampires do burn in the sun, right?" Chloe asked Francis.

"More frying, like an egg," he said. "Then, poof."

"He *could* be useful," Justin whispered to

Chloe and Malik. "Our own tour guide, to the supernatural."

Malik shook his head. "Just remember, if he winds up dating your sister, your fault," he told Chloe. "And if I fail math on Monday—"

"What?" Chloe said. "I'm great at math! I'll help you study. Why didn't you ask?"

"Or," Justin said. "Ask the vampire. I hear they're good at counting."

CHAPTER ELEVEN
New Arrivals

Malik was almost positive he'd passed math.

He just wasn't going to admit to Chloe how much she'd helped.

The kidnapped high schoolers didn't remember anything. It was unfair, how they were all in trouble. Everyone thought they'd been partying. Goofing off, running away.

But at least they were home. Everyone was safe. No one got turned into a vampire. And the dangerous vampires were gone.

The Z Team thought so, anyway. They'd biked to check out the bridge the next day. Some birdseed—and some dust—blew in the wind.

They held a movie night at Chloe's to celebrate. No vampires invited.

Francis was setting up his own place somewhere.

"Apparently," Chloe said, "he followed the bats to their cave."

"A bat cave?" Justin said. "He's actually going to live in a bat cave? Is he bringing his car?"

Malik almost spit out his soda laughing.

"What's so funny?" El asked. She'd brought them popcorn.

"Nothing," Chloe said. "Hey, do you have a second date planned with that guy—"

"It wasn't a date!" El said. "Jeez! Who doesn't have a phone, anyway? It's weird."

"Yeah!" Chloe said, relieved. "You're way too cool for a v…that guy."

"I know, right," El said. She glanced at their movie choices. "I recommend this one," she said, tapping it. "Vampire hunters are always cooler than actual vampires."

Chloe grinned at the boys. "I know, right?" she said.

Malik had been up late studying. He dozed off during the movie.

He woke up to the sound of a train whistle.

Justin and Chloe were already at the window.

A green light was on inside Zephyr Terminal. The warning light. Like the first time.

There was nothing to see, though. Only hear.

Something invisible coming to town on the Eerie Express.

Want to Keep Reading?

Turn the page for a sneak peek
at the next book in the series.

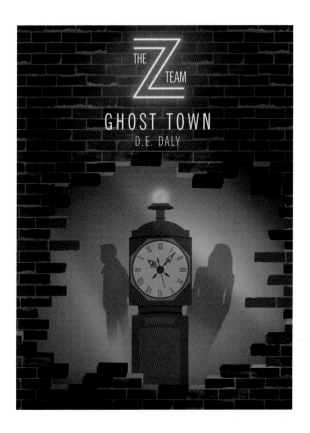

ISBN: 9781538381915

CHAPTER ONE
Headquarters

You're invited to Z Team Headquarters today!

You mean your basement?

It's a boring basement, but it's much cooler to say Headquarters.

Come over. You'll see.

Malik's basement was where he, Justin, and Chloe had figured out how to stop zombies. Where the three of them had made lists of suspected vampires.

Still, it had been a boring basement. It had concrete floors. The lights were just bulbs, hanging.

Malik had spent the past weeks making it awesome. He'd gotten free carpet samples. Made a patchwork rug. He'd gotten brighter light bulbs, new lamps. He'd hung string lights above the posters he'd put up. There was a whiteboard with markers. Three "desks" made of tray tables and chairs. A little bookshelf, with old books on Zephyr Terminal. Even his parents' extra TV.

His parents were at work a lot. So he'd done it all by himself.

Watching his friends check out their new hangout was worth it.

"Okay, this is great," Chloe said. "You even put up a *Sunny the Monster Masher* poster!"

"Who wants snacks?" Malik's mom called from upstairs.

"We're fine, Mom!" Malik called back.

"Better than fine," Chloe said. "The Z Team's all *official*."

"Let's get down to business, then," Justin said. He wrote "Mystery Train" on the whiteboard. "But first—" He held up his hand to Malik. "High-five!"

Over a month ago, they'd broken into

Bridgeside's closed train station, Zephyr Terminal, to check out a strange green warning light. Zombies and vampires had come to town on trains, through a weird portal. The Z Team got rid of both.

Now the warning light was back. Twice a week, the light turned on. A train whistle blew. At exactly midnight. Leaving the station one night. Returning another.

"Like it's making pickups and drop-offs," Malik said.

ABOUT THE AUTHOR

D.E. Daly can sometimes be found in her hometown of East Aurora, New York, a village full of haunted history and old railroad tracks. She studied writing in New Orleans and drifts back there once in a while for more of the city's magic and music. She is always chasing her next story—except the times when the story chases her.

THE Z TEAM

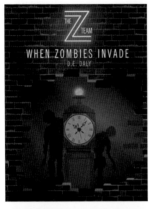

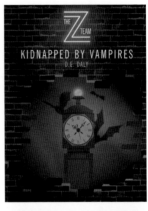

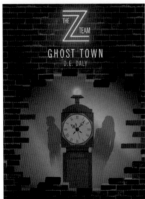

Check out more books at:

www.west44books.com

An imprint of Enslow Publishing

WEST 44 BOOKS™